IMPROVE YOUR

TENNIS SKILLS

Anita Ganeri

Tennis consultant: **David Lloyd,**
(Professional coach and former British Davis Cup team player)

Designed by **Stephen Wright**

Illustrated by **Joe McEwan** and **Kuo Kang Chen**

Additional illustrations by **Paddy Mounter** and **Guy Smith**

Photographs by **Bob Martin** (All-Sport UK)

Models: **Hedley Grist** and **Ana Alvarez**

Editorial assistance from **Emma Fischel**

This book was produced in association with Slazenger.

Contents

First published in 1989 by Usborne Publishing Ltd, 20 Garrick Street, London, WC2E 9BJ, England. Copyright © 1989 Usborne Publishing Ltd.

Printed in Belgium.

Using this book

To play good tennis, you need to be able to rely on your basic strokes. This book uses step-by-step photos to show you exactly how to play each shot, and there are clear instructions on finding the appropriate grip.

Memorize each sequence before trying it out on court. Keep checking the instructions until you get the stroke right.

To improve further, try out the practice ideas suggested on each double page.

Once you have mastered basic groundstrokes, you can move on to trickier shots like the lob. You can also learn how to add spin to the ball.

Practice boxes

You can easily spot practice boxes because they are highlighted with a yellow flash along the top.

Using tactics

Once you start playing matches you will find that winning is not just about good strokes; you also need to outwit your opponent. In this book there is lots of advice on evaluating your opponent's and your own strengths and weaknesses, and how to adapt your play accordingly.

Diagrams like this ▶ one show possible sequences of play you can use to win a point.

◀ You can learn about how to signal your plans to your partner in a doubles match without letting either of your opponents see.

See page 39 to find out how professionals get into a winning frame of mind.

Right- or left-handed?

The instructions in this book for playing strokes are given for right-handed players but can be reversed for left-handers.

Left-handers used to be encouraged to play right-handed. For example, the left-hander Maureen Connolly was playing right-handed when she became the first woman to win the Grand Slam* in 1953.

Today, however, there are many famous left-handed players, such as Martina Navratilova and John McEnroe, and people are encouraged to play left-handed if they prefer.

*See page 34 for more about the Grand Slam.

About tennis

The game of tennis which is played today comes from the ancient indoor game of 'real' or 'royal' tennis (see below). During the 19th century, people experimented with different versions of real tennis which could be played outside. Some of these became very popular and were the forerunners of modern tennis.

Tennis history

1872 First known lawn tennis club founded.

1874 Major Walter Clopton Wingfield introduced a very popular version of tennis which he called 'sphairistike' or 'sticky' for short. This formed the basis of today's game.

1875 First standard set of rules drawn up.

1877 The All-England Croquet Club became the All-England Croquet and Lawn Tennis Club. In July it held the first Wimbledon championships (men's singles only). Twenty-two players took part; the winner was Spencer William Gore. Court measurements were standardized (see pages 6–7).

1878 Overarm service first used.

1881 First US championships held (men's singles and doubles).

1882 Net lowered from 1.5m high at the posts and only 1m in the middle to its present height (see page 7).

1884 First men's doubles and first women's singles played at Wimbledon.

1887 First women's singles played at the US championships.

1891 First French championships held.

1896 Tennis was part of the first modern Olympic Games and of every Games until 1924. Reintroduced in 1988 Games.

1900 First Davis Cup match held. It was between Britain and the USA.

1905 First Australian championships held.

1913 First women's and mixed doubles played at Wimbledon.

1922 Seeding first introduced at the US championships (see page 33). Wimbledon changed from a challenge tournament (in which the previous year's champion automatically played in the final) to a knock-out tournament.

1968 'Open' tennis began (see next page).

1970 Tie-break introduced to prevent long sets (see page 33).

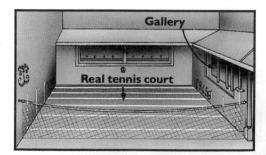

Real tennis

Real tennis is played over a net, like modern tennis, but the court also has 'galleries' or ledges around its walls. These are used as part of the playing area, like the walls in a squash court. Real tennis was first played in France in the 13th century and was popular with the aristocracy. It spread to Britain and was at its most popular in the 18th century.

Gallery

Real tennis court

The origins of scoring

The scoring system used in tennis today is based on the system used in real tennis. The number 60 was divided into four and the points in a game were 15, 30, 45 and 60. As 45 was a difficult number to say in old French, it was soon replaced with 40 as used today. The word 'love' (meaning 'zero') comes from an old English saying 'love or nothing'.

You can find more about scoring on pages 32-33.

Amateurs and professionals

Until 1968, people who played tennis for money (called professionals) could not

play in the same tournaments as unpaid players (amateurs). Only amateurs could play at Wimbledon, for example.

In 1968 tennis became an 'open' sport. This meant that anyone could play in major tournaments if the standard of their tennis was high enough.

Today all top tennis players are professionals.

Tennis millionaires

For today's top players, tennis is a well-paid, full-time job. In addition to prize money from tournaments, players can earn a lot from advertising clothes, rackets and so on.

Ivan Lendl in 1982 and Martina Navratilova in 1984 each earned over £1 million ($2 million) in prize money.

Racket revolution

In the last 20 years tennis rackets have changed a great deal. Although the shape and size has not altered much, new materials for frames, such as metal, graphite and fibreglass have replaced wood.

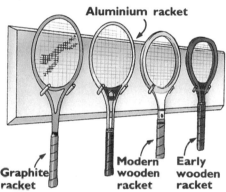

Aluminium racket

Graphite racket

Modern wooden racket

Early wooden racket

This has led to top-level tennis being played with more power and speed, favouring the more aggressive style of serve and volley play (see page 26). There is more about the different types of racket on pages 40-41.

Tennis words

Many words used in tennis have historical origins. Here are a few of them:

In real tennis, a servant tossed up the ball for the server, thus doing him a 'service'.

'Deuce' means that the score is 40-40 and one player must win two points in a row to win. It comes from the old word for 'two' on a dice.

'Tennis' comes from the old French word 'tenez' (meaning 'look out'). In real tennis, the server shouted this to his opponent as he hit the ball.

'Rally' comes from the French for 'rest' or 'revive'. In real tennis rallies were called rests because this was when the servant rested.

The court

Tennis is played on many different surfaces nowadays, but all courts are rectangular and identical in size. The court is divided in two by a net, with markings to show where the service must go, where the boundaries are for singles and doubles play and so on.

Crazy court

The hour-glass shaped court below* was used for the 19th century game of 'sticky' (see page 4). The net was placed across the narrowest part of the hour-glass shape.

Net post

Tramlines. These are used for doubles play to give a bigger court area.

Singles sidelines

Doubles sidelines

Centre service line

Service line

If a service hits the net and goes out, a 'fault' is called.

Dimensions of the court

The diagram on the right shows the dimensions of a tennis court. These have been the same for about the last 100 years.

The marker lines dividing the court are normally white or yellow. The centre service lines have to be 5cm wide. All other lines are 2.5-5cm wide but the baseline can be up to 10cm wide.

Centre mark

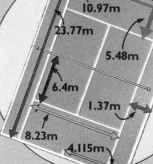

10.97m

23.77m

5.48m

6.4m

1.37m

8.23m

4.115m

*Reproduced by permission of the Wimbledon Lawn Tennis Museum.

The net

The net stretches across the centre of the court, supported at either end by posts standing 0.91m from the singles or doubles sidelines. It is higher at the ends (1.07m) than in the middle (0.91m).

A cord covered in white tape runs across the top of the net to support it. This is known as the net cord.

If a service hits the net cord but lands in the correct box, a 'let' is called and another service is allowed.

Baseline

In doubles, the net posts are moved to 0.91m outside the doubles sidelines.

Right court

Net cord

Left court

A service from the right-hand side of the court must land in the left-hand box, and vice versa.

Different surfaces

Tennis was originally played only on grass but today surfaces range from cement and clay (outdoors) to wood and carpet (indoors). Players need to adapt their game to suit different surfaces – the ball bounces faster on grass, for example, than it does on clay.*

Today the only major championships still played on grass are those held at Wimbledon.

In or out?

The ball is 'in' if even part of it touches a line; it is only 'out' if the whole ball bounces outside a line.

In some tournaments, an 'electronic eye', which sends a beam along the outside edge of the service lines, is used. The beam is broken when a ball goes out, and a buzzer sounds. Players have mixed feelings about its accuracy as it is hard to align the beam perfectly with the line, so the buzzer may sound if a ball is in.

The zones of the court

Each half of the court is divided into three playing areas, known as the 'backcourt' (the baseline area), the 'forecourt' (the area between the service line and the net), and the 'midcourt' or 'no-man's land' (the area between the backcourt and the forecourt).

No-man's land is easy to get stranded in.

Forecourt

No-man's land

Backcourt

This ball is in.

This ball is out.

*See page 30 for more about this.

Getting started

Before trying the various tennis strokes, there are some basic things to remember and practise. Knowing how to hold the racket properly and how to get into a good position to play the ball, for example, will help you play shots with greater power and control.

Parts of the racket

On the right you can see what the various parts of a racket are called. You should try to hit the ball in the centre of the strings. This is called the 'sweet spot' and will give you the cleanest, most powerful shot.

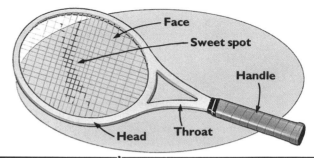

Face

Sweet spot

Handle

Head   Throat

Grips

To play a stroke well you need to hold the racket properly, altering your grip to suit the shot.

The guide on the right shows the most popular grip for each shot. To position your hand correctly for each, mark a line on your hand in the 'V' between your thumb and fingers. Next, chalk lines on the racket handle for each grip. With the racket at right angles to the ground, move your hand round until the line on it joins up with the correct line on the racket.*

Hold the racket comfortably and not too tightly.

Backhand grip

Forehand grip

Service grip

Grip the handle near the end.

Moving around the court

You often have very little time to get into the best position to play a shot, so good footwork is essential.

Try not to rush your shots.

As your feet move into position start your backswing so you are well-balanced, with your weight moving forward.

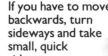

If you have to move backwards, turn sideways and take small, quick side-steps.

8   *Each grip is explained in detail with the relevant stroke.

Solo practice

Ball sense

Ball sense is as important as a good stroke technique. You need to judge where the ball will bounce to get into position to return it.

Practise this by hitting balls against a wall at various speeds. From the direction and speed at which the ball comes back, anticipate where it will bounce and how high. Watch the ball closely so you can hit it correctly.

The ready position

Between every shot, return to the 'ready' position shown on the right. You will then be able to move off quickly in any direction.

Ideally, you should stand approximately 1.5m behind the baseline to return groundstrokes and 2-3m from the net for volleys, although this will depend on how hard your opponent hits the ball.

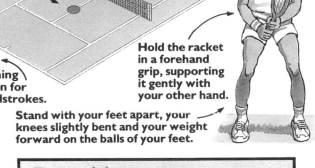

Returning position for volleys.

Returning position for groundstrokes.

Hold the racket in a forehand grip, supporting it gently with your other hand.

Stand with your feet apart, your knees slightly bent and your weight forward on the balls of your feet.

Stroke tips

You should ask yourself these five questions whichever shot you are playing:

★Am I using the right grip for the shot and keeping my wrist firm?

★Am I keeping my eye on the ball?

★Have I kept control of the racket head and face?

★Am I using the correct action to play the shot?

★Am I moving my feet properly and keeping my balance?

Types of shot

If you are right-handed, shots you play to your right are called forehands and to your left, backhands.* The three main groups of shot are:

Groundstrokes – drives (swinging action)
Overheads – service and smash (throwing action)
Volleys – played before the ball bounces (punching action)

Smash

Forehand drive

Backhand volley

*Remember, for left-handers the reverse is true.

Groundstrokes

Groundstrokes are long, powerful strokes played with a swinging action after the ball has bounced. The most common are forehand and backhand drives, which you hit down the court, usually from one baseline to the other. They are useful for returning service and for building up baseline rallies.

Try to hit groundstrokes deep, so they land as near your opponent's baseline as possible. This makes them more difficult to attack.

The forehand drive

The basic forehand drive shown below is the most commonly played shot in tennis. By developing a strong forehand you form a solid basis for the rest of your game.

1 Start in the ready position (see page 9).
2 Step to your right, turning your shoulders and feet sideways in line with the oncoming ball. With your weight on your right foot, swing your racket back quite high.

3 Keeping your eye on the ball, start swinging your racket forwards in a long, smooth action.
4 As you swing your racket at the ball, transfer your weight forwards on to your left foot.

Stroke tips

★Getting the grip right gives you better control of the racket head.

★Take your racket back as early as you can so you have plenty of time to play the shot without rushing it.

★Try to hit the ball from a comfortable distance, to give you room to swing the racket properly without overstretching.

★Correct weight transfer and good balance help you hit the ball more powerfully.

★Keep your racket head at right angles to the ground as you hit, so you don't scoop the ball up and send it out.

★Try to aim the ball about 1m above the net.

★Don't forget to follow through; if you stop the racket suddenly you may lose control of the shot.

Solo practice

Improving your forehand

To work on your forehand, hit balls against a wall. First mark a chalk line on the wall at net height, then another line 1m above. Aim shots at just above the top line.

See if you can hit ten correct shots in a row.

The forehand grip

The most popular grip used for playing forehands is the 'eastern forehand'. This is also called the 'shake-hands' grip.

To find this grip, move your hand round the handle until the line on your hand (see page 8) joins up with the line on the right-hand ridge of the racket handle.

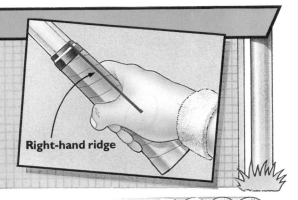

Right-hand ridge

5   **6**

5 Keeping your wrist firm, hit the ball with your racket at waist height and the racket head at right angles to the ground.
6 Continue the forward swinging action. The 'follow-through' completes the stroke action and helps control the ball.

Tennis tactics

Using groundstrokes

Groundstrokes can be played straight down the sidelines or at angles across the court. You can use them tactically as 'passing shots' to get the ball past a player who is attacking from the net. You can also use them as 'approach shots' (see page 21) to put your opponent on the defensive, giving you a chance to move in to the net to attack.

Pairs practice

Positioning
To work on your body positioning, ask a friend to hit balls to your forehand side slightly away from you. You will have to move to reach the ball, which helps you practise getting your feet and body in the right position to play the shot.

This practice also speeds up your reactions.

Star profile

Steffi Graf of West Germany has one of the best attacking forehands in the game. She hits the ball hard and fast, and the speed and agility of her footwork help her get into the perfect position to meet, attack and control the ball.

The backhand drive

To play tennis well you need to be strong on both the backhand and forehand sides. Developing a strong backhand drive gives you a greater range of possible shots to play and increases your chances of returning your opponent's shots.

1 From the ready position, turn sideways on your left foot and take your racket back, supporting it with your free hand. As you turn, change to the backhand grip.
2 When your back is almost facing the net start swinging your racket forwards, stepping in with your right foot and transferring your weight on to it.

3 Bend your knees slightly as you step forwards and swing the racket at the ball. Keep your wrist firm and swing your arm from the shoulder, not the wrist.
4 Hold the follow-through with your racket kept high and your body turned sideways to the net. Don't take your eye off the ball.

The backhand grip

To find the backhand grip, move your hand round the handle until the line on your hand joins up with the line on the left-hand ridge of the handle. This is called the 'eastern backhand' grip.

Left-hand ridge

Don't forget that you need to use different grips for forehands and backhands. To save time, try not to look at your racket as you change grip.

Solo practice

Shadow stroking

'Shadow stroking' is a way to practise groundstrokes without hitting a ball. Go through the motions of a shot, stopping to correct yourself if you are doing anything wrong.

Shadow-stroking allows you time to think about your technique.

Stroke tips

★Hitting the ball sideways-on gets your whole body - weight and power behind the shot. If you play facing the net, you only use the strength of your arm.

★To help pull your shoulders round, use your free hand to support the racket as you take it back.

★Remember to step in towards the ball with your front foot. Start moving into position early so you have plenty of time to play the shot. If you are late, you will be off-balance when you hit the ball and will lose your momentum.

★The backhand follow-through is quite high and steep.

Double-handed backhand

You can play backhands with both hands on the racket for extra control and power.

A double-handed backhand is played like a normal backhand but the left hand grips the racket just above the right hand. Most players use a backhand grip for the right hand and a forehand grip for the left, although some find using two forehand grips easier.

Tennis tactics

Baseline rallies

Baseline rallies are long exchanges of groundstrokes. You need accuracy to keep the ball in play while trying to outwit your opponent. Play shots that make your opponent run from one side of the court to the other, or hit the ball to their weakest side to force a mistake. For more about baseline play see page 26.

3 **Backhand drive across the court.**

2 **Forehand drive down the line.**

1 **Forehand drive across the court.**

4 **Backhand drive down the line.**

Pairs practice

Tramline rallies

Practising 'tramline rallies' with a friend improves your groundstroke accuracy. One of you hits forehands down the tramlines and the other returns with backhands. Start with a 10-shot rally and build up to 20 shots.

The service

Your service is the only shot in which you have complete control over the timing and positioning of the ball. Used well, it can give you a head-start by putting the receiver under pressure from the very start of a game or point, making him or her lose confidence or make errors.

The first service of a game is played from the right-hand court. From then onwards, it alternates after each point.

1 Stand sideways to the net, with your feet apart and your left foot about 10cm behind the baseline. Hold the ball in your left hand.
2 Take the racket round behind your back and throw the ball up with your left hand at the same time.

The service grip

Use the forehand grip (page 11) until you get the service action right. The best grip to use, however, is the 'chopper' grip, which helps you 'throw' your racket at the ball properly.

To find this grip, the line on your hand should join up with the line on the central plane of the handle.

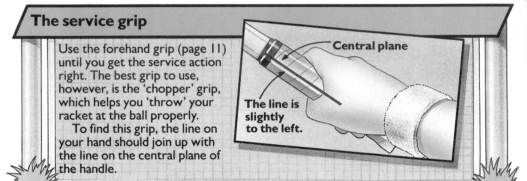

Central plane

The line is slightly to the left.

Throwing the ball up

Throwing the ball up properly makes a lot of difference to your service. Throw the ball up to the right of your left shoulder, so that if it were allowed to drop it would land about 30cm in front of your left toes.

Throw the ball up a little higher than you can reach at full stretch so you can hit it just as it starts to fall. If the throw-up is too low you might push the racket at the ball and hit it out of court; throwing too far forwards or too high means you might lose your balance by stretching for the ball.

Your feet must not touch or cross the baseline until after you have served. If they do, a 'footfault' is called. This counts as one fault or bad service.

If you get the throw-up wrong you can start again, as long as your racket has not touched the ball.

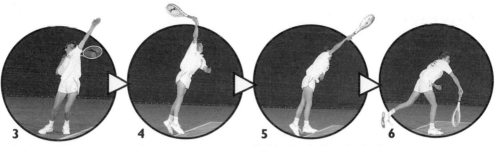

3 As you bring your racket up, start pushing up on to your toes to get your whole weight behind the shot.
4 As the racket comes over your head, flick your wrist forward to give you extra power to put into the service. Make sure you keep watching the ball as you do this.

5 Hit the ball at the highest point you can reach.
6 Follow through the service's forward momentum. Finish with the racket down your left-hand side and your weight forwards, propelling you towards the net into the ready position.

Solo practice

Hitting the target

To make your service more accurate try putting targets, such as tin cans or racket covers, in the far corners of each service court. Aim to hit each target in turn.

Stroke tips

★ To get the service action right, it helps to practise the throw-up and hit separately before putting them together.

★ If your service keeps hitting the net, check your grip and action. Remember to 'throw' the racket at the ball, not push or slap it.

★ Make sure you transfer your weight correctly from the back to the front foot so the weight and momentum carry forwards into the shot, giving it more power.

Tennis tactics

First and second services

A good first service may make your opponent rush or mis-hit the return shot. Aim to serve deep into the corners of the service court.* If the ball lands out or hits the net and lands out, you will have to rely on your second service. Most people play them slower so they are more likely to go in. Two bad services are called a 'double-fault' and you lose the point.

*See pages 24-25 for more service tactics.

Star profile

Boris Becker, one of the best servers in the game, gets great speed and power by bending then straightening his knees sharply as he throws his racket at the ball.

Playing volleys

Volleys are short, quick strokes played by punching your racket at the ball before it bounces. You put opponents under pressure by volleying because they have less time to prepare for the next shot.

Forehand volley

1   2   3   4

1 Start in the ready position (see page 9) so you will be able to move off quickly to reach the ball.
2 Turn your body so that your left shoulder is pointing at the net, with your weight resting on your right foot.

3 Step towards the ball with your left foot, transferring your weight on to it. Punch the racket at the ball, keeping the racket head up.
4 The follow-through should be short but is still important for control.

Backhand volley

1   2   3   4

1 Start in the ready position (see page 9) ready to move towards the ball.
2 Turn so that your right shoulder is pointing at the net, with your weight on your left foot.

3 Step towards the ball with your right foot. Punch the racket at the ball, keeping the racket head up.
4 Follow through in the direction of the ball for a short way.

Solo practice

Punching the ball

Chalk a circle on the wall, then stand about 2m away and volley balls at it to develop the punching action and strengthen your wrist. Try ten forehand then ten backhand volleys, stepping in and punching the ball.

Concentrate on turning your shoulders.

Tennis tactics

Going to the net

To give yourself time to move to the net to volley, play a deep shot down the line or cross-court. This forces your opponent to play a weak, defensive return which you can then volley at an angle away from your opponent for a winner.

You need good ball sense and quick reactions to volley, as there is very little time. Afterwards, get back into the ready position quickly.

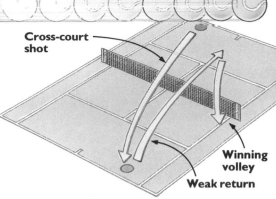

Cross-court shot

Winning volley

Weak return

Stroke tips

★Use the same grips as for your forehand and backhand drives (see pages 11 and 12) at first. As you get more confident, try the 'chopper' grip (see page 14) to save changing grips between volleys.

★It is easy to lose control of a quick volley, so keep your wrist firm and racket head steady. Squeezing the racket handle as you hit the ball helps.

★Make sure you turn your shoulders sideways to the net and transfer your weight to your front foot to give the shot power.

★Do not swing your racket when you play a volley. Keep the punching action and the follow-through short and never let the racket head drop.

Don't forget that if your racket hits the net during or after the shot, you lose the point.

Adapting the volley

Ideally, you should play a volley between shoulder and hip height, but you may need to adapt your stroke for high and low balls.

Return high volleys by hitting the ball downwards.

For low volleys, bend your knees so the ball is almost at eye-level, then punch it up.

Half-volley

You may see professionals play half-volleys. These are defensive shots and very difficult to do. The player hits the ball after it has bounced but before it reaches the top of its bounce.

Pairs practice

Hitting the target

To improve the placing of your volleys, ask a friend to hit balls to you. Try to volley them to certain target areas, for example, deep into the corners of the court or at short angles across the court.

Short angled volley

Deep volley

17

The lob and the smash

The lob and smash can be a spectacular combination, with a dramatic smash answering a high lob. These pages will help you build up a solid forehand lob and smash.

1

2

The forehand lob

Lobs are quite easy to play but you need to make sure you place the ball carefully. You should try to play a lob to make it travel high over your opponent's head, landing just inside the other baseline. The basic lob action is like the forehand drive action shown on page 10.

I Prepare to play the lob as you would a forehand drive. Take your racket back and turn on your right foot until you are sideways-on to the net.
2 Step in with your left foot, bringing your racket forward in quite a steep, low-to-high path to lift the ball.

The smash

The smash is one of the most exciting of all tennis shots to play and it can win you points outright.

You should move quickly into position under the ball and throw the racket at the ball as you would for the service, keeping your wrist as firm as possible. Hit the ball downwards hard and fast, positioning it away from your opponent if you can.

The forehand smash

1

2

I As soon as you see the lob coming, turn sideways on your right foot and start taking your racket back behind your back. Point up at the ball with your left hand to help judge its position.
2 Start bringing your racket up, ready to 'throw' it at the ball.

Tennis tactics

Using the lob

The lob is generally used defensively. A deep lob gives you time to recover your balance under pressure. It can also be used to force your opponent away from an attacking net position.

Using the smash

The smash is used to counter the lob and can be a point winner. There is no need to hit a smash as hard as you can. It is more important to concentrate on timing and placing the ball.

3 Hit the ball when it is opposite your front hip, moving your weight forward. Tilt the bottom edge of your racket slightly forward to lift the ball, using your left hand to steady you.
4 Make your follow-through really high, ending with the racket above your head.

Stroke tips

★Remember to use the same grips for lobs as for groundstrokes (see pages 11 and 12).

★Swing your racket at the ball as you would for a groundstroke.

★Transfer your weight to your front foot as you hit. Use your back foot to steady you.

★Your racket head should be low at the end of the backswing and high at the end of the follow-through.

3 Hit the ball at the highest point you can reach, jumping on your back foot and throwing your weight forward as you hit. Keep your eyes on the ball.
4 Make your follow-through long, with the racket finishing down the left-hand side of your body.

Stroke tips

★The best grip to use for the smash is the 'chopper' grip (see page 14). To start with, though, you can use your groundstroke grips if you find it easier.

★Get into position quickly by side-stepping or skipping across the court. Give yourself plenty of time to play the shot as smashes are easy to mis-hit.

★Remember to keep sideways-on to the ball.

Pairs practice

Lobs and smashes

Practising lobs and smashes with a partner is a good way to improve your control of the shots. One of you should hit up lobs and the other return them with smashes, then change round.

Try to play smashes to different parts of the court and vary their length, making some deeper and some shorter but angled. When playing lobs, vary their height and placing so your partner has to move about the court.

Lobs and smashes can also be played on the backhand side. Don't forget to change your grip and to turn your shoulders.

Using spin

When you feel confident with your basic shots you can use spin to add variety to your game. This makes the ball more difficult to return.

The shots shown here are based on the actions for groundstrokes (see pages 10-13) and the service (see pages 14-15).

Different types of spin

There are two main types of spin – topspin and slice (or underspin). They both change the way the ball travels through the air and how it bounces.*

To apply spin, you need to adjust the way you hit the ball, as shown below.

	How to hit the ball	Ball's flight path	How the ball bounces*
No spin Racket face Ground	The racket face meets the ball squarely with the racket at right angles to the ground.	The ball flies off the racket at about the same angle as it hit it, with speed but less control.	The ball bounces up at about the same angle as it hit the ground.
Topspin Hitting direction	For topspin, the racket head brushes up and over the top of the ball.	Topspin gives speed and more control. It forces the ball down so you can hit it higher (and more safely) over the net.	Topspin gives a fast, high bounce. After bouncing, the ball 'kicks' forward away from the opponent's feet.
Slice Hitting direction	For slice, the racket head brushes down and underneath the ball.	Slice takes the speed off the ball and also gives control. It makes the ball dip in the air and stay low.	Slice makes the ball skid low at the opponent's feet after it has bounced.

Topspin forehand

A topspin forehand is a reliable shot for regular use. Prepare as you would for a normal forehand drive but swing the racket up at the ball more steeply from low to high. You can hit the ball harder than normal as the spin will help to control it.

Second service

Topspin used on a second service gives extra control and reliability. It also makes the service tricky to return because the ball kicks forwards as it bounces. If you use topspin, throw the ball up slightly further to the left than normal.

*The bounce also depends on how hard the ball is hit and the type of surface (see page 30).

Sliced backhand

Prepare as you would for a normal backhand drive, but using a shorter backswing. Bring your racket forwards in a steep swing from high to low and bend your knees if you are returning a low ball. Keep your wrist firm and the follow-through low.

Approach shots

Sliced backhands are often used as 'approach shots'. These are groundstrokes played with spin to give you time to move towards the net. When your opponent hits a short ball (one that does not reach the baseline), return it with an approach shot deep into the corner of the court. You can then move quickly forwards to play a winning volley.

Touch shots

These are delicate, sliced shots needing excellent racket control. The most common is the drop shot, played on the forehand or backhand side. Drop shots are often used to break up long baseline rallies by hitting the ball from inside the baseline and aiming it to land just over the net.

Forehand drop shot

1
2
3

1 Prepare as if playing a forehand drive. Take the racket back and step across with your left leg.
2 Bring the racket forwards and brush down and under the ball.

3 Don't forget to follow through in the direction the ball is travelling.
The slice will cause the ball to fly low over the net and spin backwards from the bounce.

Pairs practice

Practising spin

You need to practise adding spin to the ball before you can use it confidently with normal groundstrokes in a rally. Ask a friend to hit balls to you and return them using a sequence of shots such as the one below.

Basic forehand drive

Sliced backhand

Topspin forehand

1
2
3

Tennis tactics

When to use spin

★Use spin to upset your opponent's rhythm in a long baseline rally. Your opponent will find it harder to anticipate your next shot.

★Use heavy topspin for better ball control, gaining accuracy without losing speed.

★Use spin to disguise shots and surprise opponents; prepare as for a groundstroke then hit the ball with topspin or slice.

★You need to use spin to reply to spin on your opponent's shots. In general, counter topspin with slice and slice with topspin.

21

Playing a match

Winning a tennis match relies as much on planning, tactics and single-mindedness as it does on good, powerful shots.

Below are some general tips for planning how to play a match.

Knowing your game

Asking yourself questions about your own game helps you work out the best match plan to exploit your strengths and cover up your weaknesses.

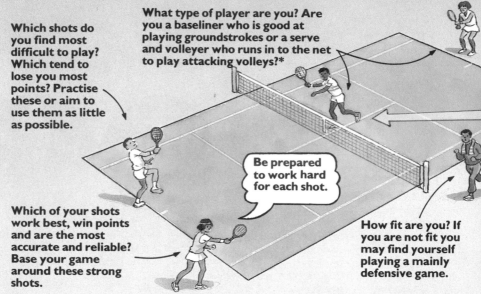

Which shots do you find most difficult to play? Which tend to lose you most points? Practise these or aim to use them as little as possible.

What type of player are you? Are you a baseliner who is good at playing groundstrokes or a serve and volleyer who runs in to the net to play attacking volleys?*

Be prepared to work hard for each shot.

Which of your shots work best, win points and are the most accurate and reliable? Base your game around these strong shots.

How fit are you? If you are not fit you may find yourself playing a mainly defensive game.

Knowing your opponents

Before matches, try to find out as much as you can about your opponents. This helps you work out the best tactics to use against them.

★What are your opponents' strengths? If they have strong forehands, avoid playing the ball to that side.

★What are their weaknesses? Concentrate on making them play their weaker shots.

★Are your opponents left- or right-handed? If you attack their backhands, for example, hit the ball to the right of left-handers and to the left of right-handers.

★Do they use double-handed backhands? Make them stretch for backhands. This forces them to release the supporting hand and makes the shot weaker.

★Are your opponents fit and strong? Make them run about to tire them out.

Coping with nerves

Feeling nervous stops you playing at your best. Relax by taking several deep breaths as you prepare to serve or return service. Think positively about winning the match.

If opponents look tense and hesitate before playing shots, use this to your advantage. Undermine their confidence further by forcing them to make mistakes (see opposite page).

See page 26 for more about these styles of play.

Tennis tactics

Match play tips

★ After shots, return to a central position so you can cover both sides of the court. In baseline play, return to the centre of the baseline. If you are volleying, stand about 3m from the centre line of the net, ready to move forwards if necessary.

★ If you are not sure which shot to play next, play one you feel comfortable with.

★ If your opponent plays well and puts you under pressure, just aim to keep the ball in play until you can get the advantage back.

Outwitting your opponent

To win a tennis match, you need to outwit and surprise opponents as well as outpowering them.

Vary your shots using topspin and slice (see pages 20-21).

Try to keep your opponent guessing about your next move by disguising your shots (see page 21).

Try to judge what sort of shot your opponent will hit next so you can get into a good position to return it.

Vary where you place the ball. Hit some shots at angles cross-court and some straight down the lines.

Another way of outwitting opponents is to wrong-foot them. Start with a regular hitting pattern. Then, as your opponent moves to anticipate your next shot, hit it in the opposite direction.

Unforced errors

Many points are lost by one player making more avoidable mistakes than the other, for example, through lack of concentration or lack of control.* These are called 'unforced errors'.

In the 1977 Wimbledon final, Bjorn Borg beat Jimmy Connors in the final set. Connors made 70 unforced errors against Borg's 16.

Working out a match plan

Work out beforehand how you would like the match to go. Think how you will return service, deal with different service returns and so on. Keep your match plan flexible and be prepared to alter it if it is not working.

Keep a record of your match plan to compare it with your actual performance.

Match plan   PAGE 1

Opponent has weak, sliced backhand. Attack backhand with service. Take advantage of weak, defensive return to get to the net to volley.

*See pages 31 and 39 for tips on improving your concentration.   23

Service tactics

Serving and returning service are two of the most important shots in tennis. They can immediately put you in a strong position – or give your opponent the advantage if you play them badly. Below are some tips on how to make the most of the two shots.

Where to stand

As the server, you have a big tactical advantage. By serving well, you can immediately put your opponent on the defensive and under pressure.

The diagrams below show where to serve from to exploit a right-handed* opponent's backhand, usually a player's weaker shot.

Serving in singles

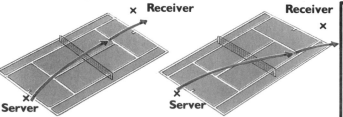

x Receiver

Receiver
x

Server

Server

Serving from the right: stand just behind the baseline, right of the centre mark. Serve almost straight down the centre line.

Serving from the left: stand just behind the baseline, left of the centre mark. Aim for the far right of the service box.

Serving in doubles

In doubles you should stand midway between the centre mark and the doubles sidelines. This means you can get quickly into position at the net. See page 27 for more about doubles positions.

Serving to the forehand

If your opponent has a weak forehand, take advantage of it. Aim your service wide to the forehand to force your opponent out of position, creating an opening for your next shot.

Tennis tactics

Serving tips

★Concentrate on serving accurately rather than very fast. Try to get at least two-thirds of your first services in.

★To keep your opponent guessing, vary your serving: aim a high percentage of services at your opponent's backhand, but occasionally serve wide to the forehand.

★You need to be able to rely on your second service, so serve more slowly to make sure the ball goes in. Try using topspin (see page 20).

★Deep services force your opponent to play weak, high returns; serving short gives your opponent the chance to play strong, winning returns.

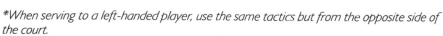

24 *When serving to a left-handed player, use the same tactics but from the opposite side of the court.

Returning service

Returning service well is just as important as good serving. To win a match, you need to win at least one of your opponent's service games in each set. This is known as 'breaking the service'.

Where to stand

Where you stand and what type of return you play will be affected by the speed of your opponent's service, but here are some basic guidelines for both singles and doubles.

Singles

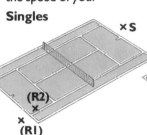

Doubles

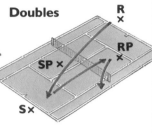

For a fast first service, stand about 1m behind the baseline (R1). Move forward slightly for a second service (R2).

In doubles, a good return can force your opponent (S) to play a weak shot which your partner (RP) can volley for a winner.

Taking advantage

Try to judge whether the server intends to stay back on the baseline or come to the net after serving. If he or she is likely to run forwards, play the ball low over the net to force an awkward, low return. If he or she stays back, play a deep, higher shot.

Tennis tactics

Returning tips

★Be prepared to react quickly to the service – a ball travelling at 96km/h will reach you in just one second. Some top male players serve at 193km/h.

★You may need to move backwards or forwards, so keep your knees and body slightly bent with your weight forwards.

★Tempt the server to make mistakes by returning reliably.

Types of return

Below are examples of different types of return you can use.

Blocked and chipped returns

These are adaptations of normal groundstroke returns. They have short backswings which give you more time to play the shot.

Blocked returns are good against fast services.

'Punch' the racket at the ball after it has bounced.

Chipped returns are good against high, topspin services.

Hit the ball firmly with slice.

Lob return

In doubles, try lobbing the return high over the server's partner's head. This may win the point outright or force your opponents back to the baseline.

Singles tactics

Below are some singles tactics to try. You can apply them to the two main styles of play – baseline play and serve and volley play.

Baseline play

In baseline play games are made up mainly of long groundstroke rallies from the baseline. The idea is to keep the ball in play as long as you can to force your opponent to make mistakes, or until you see an opportunity for a winning shot.

Catching your opponent out

★ Vary your shots to catch your opponent off-balance. Try going cross-court or down the line.

★ Change your shot length. A short, angled shot (see blue arrow) may force your opponent to one side. You can then play a winning shot.

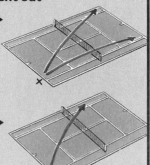

★ If your opponent likes to play at the net, a high lob might make him or her hesitate before moving forwards on the next point.

> ### General tips
>
> ★ Don't try to hit every shot hard; this can easily lead to mistakes or unforced errors (see page 23).
>
> ★ Concentrate on manoeuvring your opponent out of position by making him or her move about the court as much as you can.
>
> ★ Always try to hit your shots deep until you can create an opening for a winning shot.
>
> ★ Return to the baseline between shots so you can cover both sides easily.

Serve and volley tactics

In serve and volley play you follow your service in to the net to play attacking volleys. Below are two ways to get to the net. Once you decide to go there, move as quickly as possible. Don't change your mind or you could be stranded half-way.

Player A

1 Serves and moves in towards net.
3 Plays first volley deep into corner of court. Moves in to net.
5 Plays winning volley.

Player B

2 Plays quite good, low return.
4 Plays weak, high return.

▲ Option 1

Option 2 ▼

Player A

1 Plays deep, fast service; moves straight to net.
3 Hits winning volley away from opponent.

Player B

2 Plays weak, high return.

Doubles tactics

Good doubles tactics begin before the ball is in play, when you choose your starting positions. Doubles is mainly an attacking, serve and volley game, so you need to get to the net fast.

Positions on court

On the right you can see where players normally stand to start a point when the service is from the right court.* After this point, the server (S) and partner (SP) change sides. The receiver (R) moves forwards and his partner (RP) moves back to return service, as shown by the arrows.

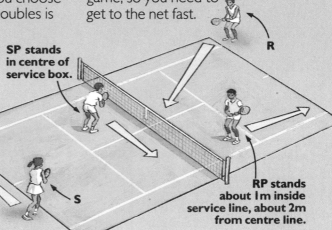

SP stands in centre of service box.

RP stands about 1m inside service line, about 2m from centre line.

Changing formation

Players may decide to alter their starting positions if some of their opponents' shots are particularly strong. Here are two options:

1 Australian formation

The server's partner moves across to stand in the server's half of the court. The server stands close to the centre mark to serve, then moves quickly across to cover the empty half of the court.

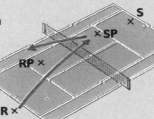

If R has a very strong cross-court service return, SP is now in a better position to volley it.

2 Defensive formation

Both players in the receiving team stand on the baseline to receive the service. They stay there until they see an opportunity to move in to the net.

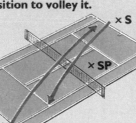

This may be used if S is very strong, forcing R to play defensive returns.

Going to the net

The aim of both doubles teams is to get to the net as quickly as possible and attack. This forces their opponents back to defend from the baseline.

Reflex volleys

In top-class matches, you may see all four players volleying at the net. These net rallies are so fast that volleys are often played just by instinct. These are known as 'reflex volleys'.

*There is more about serving and receiving positions on pages 24-25.

Playing as a team

Doubles is based on teamwork, so make sure you get on well with your partner and can encourage each other. Find someone whose game complements yours so you can cover the court effectively.

Below is a way to find a suitable partner. First give various aspects of your game marks out of five, then do the same for a friend. The ideal total across each row should be between seven and ten.

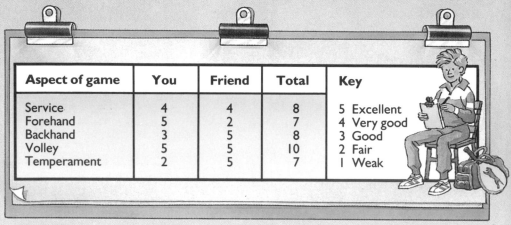

Aspect of game	You	Friend	Total	Key
Service	4	4	8	5 Excellent
Forehand	5	2	7	4 Very good
Backhand	3	5	8	3 Good
Volley	5	5	10	2 Fair
Temperament	2	5	7	1 Weak

Assessment

This would be a good combination. Your partner has a stronger backhand than yours so should cover the left-hand side of the court, while you use your excellent forehand in the right-hand court. As you are both good volleyers you should be able to form a strong attacking force at the net.

Star spotting

Try this test to see if you would make a good partner for a top-class player. Below are marks for Ivan Lendl. Add your own marks to these.

Aspect of game	Score
Service	5
Forehand	5
Backhand	5
Volley	3
Temperament	5

Assessment

Volleys are Lendl's slightly weak point so you would need to be strong at the net. Lendl's groundstrokes are strong so he should take the lead in baseline rallies.

Teamwork strategy

Covering your partner

Always stay alert while your partner is playing the ball; be ready to cover the rest of the court and hit the shot if he or she misses it.

Intercepting

As the server's partner, you mainly cover half the forecourt. You could also move across and intercept cross-court service returns with a forehand volley.

Feinting

Use feinting to confuse your opponents. Move slightly, as if about to intercept, then move back again while your partner plays the shot.

Communication

To play well as a team it is essential to communicate with your partner. You can call out or use signals so you both know what to do and where to move to.

Calling

To avoid getting in each other's way or both leaving a ball, work out a system of simple calls like those below.

★ 'Mine' – you have more chance to hit a good shot than your partner.

★ 'Yours' – your partner has more chance of hitting a good shot.

★ 'Out' – your opponent's shot looks as if it is going out.

★ 'Cross' – you need to swop sides of the court.

Balls down the centre line are usually taken by whoever can play a forehand.

Signalling

Signals can be used to tell your partner what you are going to do. If you are the server's partner, make hand signals behind your back to indicate that you intend to intercept the return or stay put.

This stops your opponents guessing your next move.

Star profile

Many successful doubles pairs have one left-handed and one right-handed player, for example Martina Navratilova (who is left-handed) and Pam Shriver (right-handed). Left-handers normally play in the left court so both players can return service using forehands.

29

Adapting your game

To be a good match player you need to adapt your game to suit the playing conditions. Here you can see how to play in difficult weather and the best type of game to use on different surfaces.

Weather watch

Wind behind you

Get into position early to play the ball.

Playing into the wind

Hit the ball harder than normal.

Serving in bright sunshine

If your opponent is playing into the sun, play high lobs so the ball is difficult to see.

Problem Your shots fly through the air faster, so you need extra control to stop them going out.

Solution Hit the ball quite gently and with topspin for more control.

Problem Your shots travel very slowly through the air but your opponent's travel very fast.

Solution To fight the wind, use slice to keep the ball low over the net.

Problem It can be hard to see the ball when you toss it up to serve.

Solution Use a slower service into the sun so your eyes can recover before your next shot.

Different surfaces

Different court surfaces change the way the ball bounces, so you need to adapt your game accordingly. The chart shows what happens on 'fast' and 'slow' courts.

Speed of court	Types of surface	Type of game	Techniques
Fast courts The ball bounces low and fast. It skids forwards after bouncing.	Grass Cement Some indoor carpet courts Artificial grass	You will be most successful using a serve and volley game (see page 26).	You have little time to play shots, so try to make your backswing shorter.
Slow courts The ball bounces slowly. It comes off the ground at a steep angle.	Clay All-weather (tarmac) courts Rubber indoor courts	You will find it is most effective to use baseline play. (see page 26).	With more time to prepare for shots, try putting topspin on your groundstrokes.

Being positive

A winning player needs a positive attitude, good concentration, confidence to back up sound shots and physical fitness.

Setting yourself goals

To improve your game and self-confidence, you need to set yourself goals to achieve. As you reach each goal, aim for another slightly harder one. Try writing down your targets and ways of reaching them, as shown below.

Task	Practice	Goal 1	Goal 2
To improve accuracy of backhand drive	Aim backhands at a racket cover placed about 1m in from the baseline and sideline.	Aim to hit the target at least 1 out of 25 times. Don't worry if it is hard at first.	Aim to hit the target about 1 out of 15 times. Keep trying to improve further.
To improve service	Aim at targets put near each corner of the service court.	Try to hit the targets at least 1 out of 25 times.	Try to hit the targets about 1 out of 15 times.

Thinking to win

Force yourself to play one point at a time. Thinking back over lost points or mistakes discourages you.

Getting distracted or losing your temper can cost you points. Stay calm and concentrate on your next stroke.

If you lose a match, decide which parts of your game let you down, then practise them.

Your opponent is probably nervous too, so create problems for him or her and forget yours.

Solo practice

Concentration drill

Try this exercise to help you concentrate during long rallies. Say to yourself: 'hit' as your opponent hits the ball; 'bounce' as the ball bounces on your side; and 'hit' as you hit the ball.

Hit

Bounce

Scoring

Below you can find out about the scoring system used in tennis and see some practical examples of how it works.*

Game...

The points are 15, 30, 40, then game. To win a game, you must win these four points by a margin of two points. If the score reaches 40-40, or 'deuce', the next point scored is 'advantage'. Again you need a two-point lead to win the game.

Set...

The first player to win six games by a margin of at least two games, for example, 6-4, wins the set. If the score reaches 6-6, the tie-break is used (see next page).

Scoring in a game

Below is an example of how the points in a game might be scored. Player A is serving.

Player A	Player B	Winner of point
15	0	A
15	15 (15 all)	B
30	15	A
30	30	B
40	30	A
40	40 (deuce)	B
40	A (advantage B)	B
	Game	B

...and Match

To win a match, you normally have to win the best of three sets. Men play the best of five sets in major tournaments and in the Davis Cup.

The scoreboard

The picture below shows the type of scoreboard you might see at a major championship. A men's singles match is in progress.

The score was 5-5, so Volley had to win two more games.

Lights indicate which player is serving.

Games and points in the set being played.

In a game the server's score is called out first, so this would be 'love-40'.

Set numbers are shown below the score in the set.

If Volley wins the next point and the game, it will be a 'love game' because the opponent has failed to score anything.

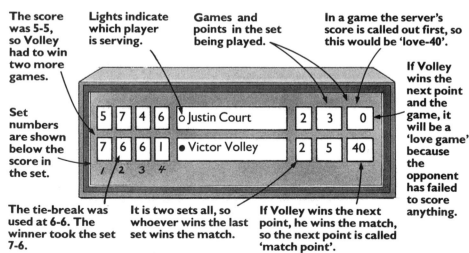

The tie-break was used at 6-6. The winner took the set 7-6.

It is two sets all, so whoever wins the last set wins the match.

If Volley wins the next point, he wins the match, so the next point is called 'match point'.

The winner's score is called out first, so if Volley wins this game, he will have won by 7-5, 6-7, 6-4, 1-6, 6-3; by a margin of three sets to two.

The tie-break

Tie-breaks were introduced to stop sets becoming too long. They are played when the score in games reaches 6-6.

Points are scored as 1,2,3,4 and so on. The first player to win seven points with a margin of at least two points wins the tie-break and the set. If the score in points is 6-6, play continues until one player has a two-point lead. A tie-break is not used in the final set.

The player who would serve first in a normal set, serves the first point of the tie-break. After this, players serve two points each.

Normally, players change ends of the court after the first game and then after every two games. In a tie-break, they change ends every six points.

The officials

Matches in major tournaments are overseen by officials who make sure that they are played fairly. Below you can see where the officials sit and what they do.

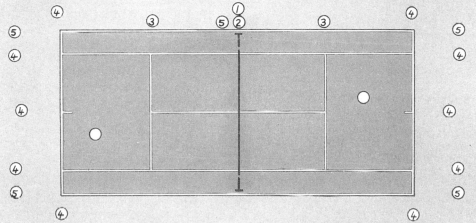

1 Umpire Sits on a 'high chair' so has good view of the court. Keeps and calls out the score and writes the details on a scoresheet. Sees that the rules are kept and can give penalties for bad behaviour. Can also overrule line judges' decisions if a 'bad call' has been made.

2 Net judge Keeps finger on the net cord during service so can feel whether the ball hits the net or not. Calls 'let' if the ball touches the net but still lands in (see pages 6-7).

3 Service line judges Look at the service line. Call if the service is out.

4 Line judges Judge whether the ball is inside or outside the line they are watching. Call if the server footfaults.

5 Ball boys and girls Collect up balls between rallies and supply players with balls for serving. They also change the balls after the first seven and then after every nine games, as they quickly become soft and lose their shape during play.

Going on tour

Top tennis professionals play in tournaments all over the world. The playing 'season' lasts all year round, so life as a full-time player is very demanding. Here you can find out about the men's and women's touring circuits and about some of the major competitions.

The men's tour

The men's tour (called the Nabisco Grand Prix) consists of over 75 tournaments around the world. Over 1,000 players take part. They must compete in at least 14 Grand Prix events a year.

The year ends with two 'Masters' tournaments (one for singles and another for doubles). Only the top eight singles players and the top eight doubles pairs qualify to take part.

The women's tour

The women's tour (called the Virginia Slims series) is run separately but along the same lines as the men's tour. It was started in 1971 and includes about 55 tournaments around the world. At the end of the year, the Virginia Slims Championships are held. Only the top 16 singles players and the top eight doubles teams qualify to take part in this tournament.

Calendar of the main tournaments

■ January	Australian Open	■ August	US Open, New York
● February	Indian Wells, USA	● September	Spanish Open
▲	German Open	▲	Tokyo, Japan
■ March	Lipton International Championships, USA	● October	Tokyo, Japan
		▲	European Indoor Championships
● April	Monte Carlo Open	▲ November	Virginia Slims Championships
▲	Houston, USA		
■ May	Italian Open	●	Nabisco Masters (singles)
■	French Open	● December	Nabisco Masters (doubles)
■ June	Wimbledon Championships		
● July	US Clay Court Championships	**Key**	● Men's event
▲	Newport, USA		▲ Women's event
			■ For men and women

Winning the Grand Slam

To win the Grand Slam, a player has to win all of the following four championships – the Australian Open, the French Open, Wimbledon and the US Open – in the same year. Very few players have ever achieved the Grand Slam. As the tournaments are played on a variety of surfaces (hard, clay and grass), the winner has to be an excellent all-rounder. The cup on the right shows the names of the Grand Slam winners so far.

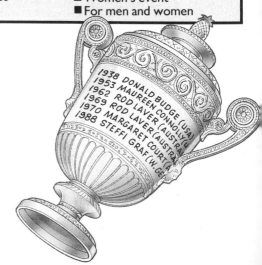

1938 DONALD BUDGE (USA)
1953 MAUREEN CONNOLLY
1962 ROD LAVER (AUSTRA
1969 ROD LAVER (A
1970 MARGARET COURT (A
1988 STEFFI GRAF (W. GE

World rankings

Players can earn points from their performance in any of the tour competitions. Bonus points can also be scored by beating better players.

The points are fed on to a computer list which shows how high each male and female player is ranked in the world.

At the end of the year, the player at the top of each of the male and female rankings is named as the world number one.

Seeding

In competitions the top quarter (or sometimes the top eighth) of players are 'seeded' according to how good they are. In most tournaments, seedings are based on the computer rankings. The number one seed will be the best player and the one who is expected to win the tournament.

The draw

To decide who plays whom, unseeded players' names are written down and drawn out of a hat. If there is an odd number of players, those left are given 'byes'. This means they go into the second round without playing a first round match.

Seeded players are given set positions in the draw to prevent them meeting until later rounds. In the semi-finals, the number one and two seeds should play the number three and four seeds, with the number one and two seeds meeting in the final.

1	**V. Volley (1)**	**V. Volley**	**V. Volley**	**V. Volley** 6-3, 6-4	Winner **V. Volley** 6-4, 7-5
2	F. Hand-Drive				
3	A.Dropshot	A.Dropshot			
4	bye		**S.Smash**		
5	**S.Smash (3)**	**S.Smash**			
6	T.Ournament				
7	S.Pin	T.Tactic			
8	T.Tactic				
9	bye	T.Racket			
10	T.Racket		**L.Lob**		
11	A.D.Vantage	**L.Lob**		**J.Court** 6-2, 7-5	
12	**L.Lob (4)**				
13	bye	A.Deuce	**J.Court**		
14	A.Deuce				
15	B.Hand-Drive	**J.Court**			
16	**J.Court (2)**				

Note: numbers in brackets indicate seeded positions

Other events

Apart from the official tour events there are many other individual and team competitions held during the year. Below is a selection.

★**Davis Cup** The most important team competition for men, first held in 1900. Over 70 countries compete yearly.

★**Federation Cup** A similar event but for women, first held in 1963. Today over 40 teams take part.

★**Olympic Games** In Seoul in 1988, tennis was reintroduced as an Olympic sport for the first time since 1924.

★**Exhibition matches** Usually 4-man competitions, with no computer points.

★**Satellite tour** Groups of tournaments which are the starting place for players trying to gain computer points.

★**Special events** Privately organized tournaments with large amounts of prize money but no ranking points.

Improving your fitness

To play good tennis you need to build up your fitness as well as your technique, using exercises such as the ones shown below. Over the page you can see how to build them into a regular training programme.

Warming up

You should always warm up before a match or training session to loosen your muscles so you do not strain them.

Repeat each exercise below five times. Hold the stretch for five seconds, being careful not to overstretch, then relax.

Stand with your feet apart ▶ and your left arm raised. Bend to the right, then straighten up slowly and repeat to the other side.

◀ Stand up straight, then bend down slowly and touch your toes. Straighten up slowly, keeping your legs straight.

Lunge to your left, bending ▶ your left knee but keeping your right leg straight. Straighten up and repeat to the right.

◀ Stand and shake out your hands and arms for a few seconds. Then rotate your arms in ten forward, then ten backward circles.

Stand with your hands on ▶ your hips. Lean back from your waist, keeping your legs straight. Then rotate your upper body in a circle.

Warming down

After a match or training session, do some of the exercises above, then jog gently for 5-10 minutes to warm down. This helps avoid aching muscles.

Your heart and pulse rate

During exercise, your heart has to pump more blood to your muscles and so beats faster. As you get fitter, your heart gets stronger and pumps more efficiently, so beats fewer times. You can tell how fast your heart is beating by taking your pulse.*

Taking your pulse

1 Press the middle fingers of one hand on the inside of your other wrist. You will feel a gentle throbbing which is your pulse.

2 Use a watch with a second hand to time how often your pulse beats in 15 seconds.

3 Multiply this by four to find your pulse rate per minute. The average rate is 70-80 beats.

Testing your fitness

By monitoring your pulse rate you can see how your fitness is improving.

★Take your pulse before you exercise, and again afterwards.

★Note the difference and time how long it takes for your pulse to return to normal. As you get fitter, the time should decrease.

Building up stamina

Running

Running is a good way of building up stamina. Start by running at a comfortable pace for 10-15 minutes, twice a week. After a while, you should find you can run much further in the same time.

Skipping

Skip fast for 30 seconds, rest for 30 seconds, then repeat.

*Your pulse rate should never go higher than 180 beats per minute.

Improving your speed and agility

Shuttle sprints

You can use shuttle sprints to build up your speed and improve the way you turn and move about the court.

Put three balls on the singles sidelines, about 10cm apart. Stand behind the opposite side-line, then sprint across the court, pick up one ball, turn quickly and sprint back. Put the ball on the sideline and repeat for the other two.

As you get fitter, increase the number of balls.

Get a friend to do the same at the other end of the court and see who is fastest.

Try timing yourself to see how much you improve.

Building up strength

Do each exercise below for 30 seconds, relax for 30 seconds, then go on to the next exercise. At first, do the whole routine 2-3 times, resting for one minute between each routine. You can increase the number of times as you improve.

Press-ups

Lie face down with your hands beneath your shoulders. Push your body up, using your arms. Bend your elbows, then lower your body almost down to the floor.

Try to keep your body straight.

Sit-ups

Lie on your back, your hands clasped behind your neck and your knees bent. Sit up, bring your elbows down to touch your knees, then lower your body again.

It may help if someone holds your feet.

Step-ups

Step up on to a stair or low bench and step down again. Alternate the leg you lead with.

Gradually increase your speed.

Back arch

Lie on your stomach with your hands, palms up, by your side. Slowly raise your upper body and legs off the floor.

You should stop if you feel any pain in your back.

Knee jumps

Stand with your feet together and jump up, bringing your knees up to your chest. Do this twice, then rest and repeat.

You might find it easier to start from a crouching position.

Squat jumps

Crouch down, your hands either side of your knees. Thrust your legs backwards so your legs and body are straight. Jump forwards again, bringing your knees up to your elbows.

Keep your hands in the same position as you jump.

Training programme

The training programme below is based on the exercises shown on pages 36-37.

The programme is divided into three stages. As you get fitter and start finding the first stage easy, go on to the next and so on. Be careful not to overdo it, though, and make sure you warm up before you start the programme and warm down when you finish. Try to do the whole programme twice a week.

Exercise	Stage 1	Stage 2	Stage 3
Running	10-15 minutes	15-20 minutes	20-25 minutes
Skipping	5 repeats	10 repeats	15 repeats
Shuttle sprints	3 balls in 13 seconds	6 balls in 27 seconds	9 balls in 40 seconds
Strength (whole routine)	2-3 times	4 times	5 times

Injuries

Tennis players can suffer from many types of injury; below are some of the most common. For injuries other than minor cuts and bruises, always consult your doctor.

Injury	Treatment
Blisters. Caused by socks or shoes rubbing against your skin, or by gripping your racket too tightly.	Pierce blister with a sterilized needle and press the fluid out with cotton wool. Do not remove top of blister.
Sprains. Damage to ligaments supporting the bones in your joints. May happen if you fall awkwardly.	Treat with ice-pack (wrap some ice in a damp towel) to reduce the swelling. Bandage area and rest it.
Pulled muscles. Muscles and tendons may tear or strain if you overstretch or move awkwardly.	Use ice-pack to reduce the swelling, then rest area. If the injury continues to hurt, consult your doctor.
Tennis elbow. Inflamed elbow; sometimes caused by constantly mis-timing your shots.	Might need physiotherapy to get muscles and joints working properly.

Avoiding injury

★Always warm up properly (see page 36). 'Cold' muscles easily strain or tear.

★Build up your training slowly. Don't try to do too much to start with.

★Make sure you have a balanced diet. Leave at least two hours between eating and playing a match to avoid the risk of stomach cramp or indigestion.

★If you feel pain, stop exercising. Treat injuries as soon as they happen to prevent further damage. Allow plenty of time for injuries to heal. With serious injuries, consult your doctor before training or playing again.

★If your knees, ankles or elbows are weak, you can wear support bandages (available from sports shops or chemists). Put the support on about ten minutes before exercise and take it off afterwards.

Mental preparation

Being mentally prepared for a match is essential. Professional players work hard at getting themselves into a calm, winning frame of mind before a match and at remaining relaxed during a match.

Before a match

If you feel nervous or tense before a match you will find it hard to play at your best. Below are two simple exercises, based on yoga and meditation techniques, which you can use to help calm you down.

1 To relax your muscles, lie on the floor with your head on a pillow and your arms loosely by your sides. Close your eyes and take a couple of deep breaths. Then relax every muscle in your body, including your eyelids and mouth. Do this for 5-10 minutes, then roll over on to your side and get up slowly.

2 Meditation helps clear your mind so you feel calmer. Sit comfortably in a quiet room. Close your eyes and concentrate on a word, such as 'relax'. Repeat this word to yourself every time you breathe out. Try not to get distracted; if you do, focus your attention immediately on the word again. Do this for about 20 minutes a day.

Building confidence

Many players have coaches who discuss tactics with them and encourage them to think positively before a match. Sometimes players also listen to 'psych-up' tapes to boost their confidence.

Some players use sports psychologists who devise programmes of exercises to suit the individual player's needs.

Keeping your cool on court

Relaxation and concentration are just as important during a match, particularly if it is very long or you feel under pressure. These tips will help you keep on top form.

★Learn to co-ordinate your breathing with hitting the ball. Breathing out relaxes the muscles, so aim to breathe out as you hit the ball.

★If you are getting tense, shake out your shoulders and arms, and roll your neck from side to side.

★Make a conscious effort to slow your game down if you are under pressure and making mistakes by rushing.

★Settle into a routine before serving. Some players juggle or bounce the balls a set number of times to prevent rushing the service.

★To avoid being distracted, especially between points, keep your head down and concentrate on your racket strings.

★During rallies, concentrate on the seams of the ball to keep all of your attention focused on the point.

★Play one point at a time; try not to worry about what has happened or what might happen.

Tennis kit

Tennis clothes and rackets are available in a wide range of styles. On these two pages there are tips to help you choose the equipment you need. Most sports shops are also happy to offer advice.

Choosing a racket

Choosing a racket is very personal. Not only does it depend on your size and strength, it must also suit your particular style of play. Here are three things to think about:

I What is it made of?

Tennis rackets used to be made from wood, but today many different materials are used including aluminium, fibreglass and graphite.

If you like playing an attacking serve and volley game, a stiff racket of aluminium or all-graphite is best. If you prefer delicate play, a more flexible, composite (a graphite and nylon mixture, for example) racket is better.

2 How heavy is it?

Rackets come in a variety of weights, shown in the table below. In general, the stronger you are, the heavier a racket you can use. Light rackets are best for 11-13 year olds and light medium for 14-16 year olds.

Light	up to 369g
Light medium	369-383g
Medium	383-397g
Top	Over 397g

★ Try a few practice strokes with the racket. It should not feel top heavy.

3 How big is the grip?

The size of the racket handle varies: the heavier the racket is, the bigger the grip. You need to find a comfortable grip. If it is too big, the racket will slip in your hand as you hit the ball; if it is too small, your hand will be very cramped. If you like the racket weight but find the grip too small, you can buy extra binding for the handle.

★ To find the correct grip size for you, hold the racket comfortably. Your thumb and second finger should overlap slightly.

Head sizes

There are three sizes of racket head – normal, mid-size and jumbo. Mid-size and jumbo rackets give a bigger 'sweet spot' (see page 8), but you have less control with the bulkier jumbo size. Most top players use mid-size rackets.

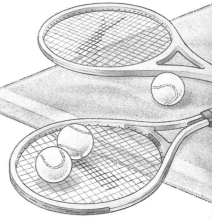

Strings and tension

Strings are made from natural gut (sheep's intestines) or from synthetic materials. Top players prefer gut as it gives better control but cheaper, synthetic strings last longer.

Rackets can be strung to different tensions. The rackets sold in sports shops are strung to medium tension. In general, tighter strings give more power but less control.

★ To test the tension, pluck one of the lengthwise strings near the racket handle. Tight strings will make a 'pinging' noise.

Grip coverings

The grip is usually covered in a synthetic leather-like material which absorbs moisture and stops your hand slipping. You should change the grip covering regularly. Professional players often change the grip covering five or six times during one match.

Balls

Tennis balls are made of rubber, clay and other materials, and are covered with fabric. Good tennis balls are pressurized (that is, air is sealed inside them) so they bounce correctly. With use, however, the air escapes and the balls become softer. This changes their bounce so they need replacing.

Always try to use good quality balls, preferably officially tested ones.

★To test a ball, drop it on the floor from about head height. It should bounce high and straight.

A towel is good for wiping sweat off your hands and racket handle.

Carry your gear in a sports bag.

Choosing a tennis outfit

Your clothes and shoes should feel comfortable and allow you to move about court easily.

Clothes

White is the traditional colour for tennis clothes but pastel colours are often worn today. It is probably best to buy mainly white clothes, though, as some clubs may not allow coloured clothing.

Cotton clothes are better than man-made ones as they absorb sweat.

Socks

Thick, towelling socks are best for comfort and support. On a hard court, you could try wearing two pairs of socks for extra cushioning.

Sweatbands

Elasticated towelling bands for your wrists and head are useful in hot weather for soaking up sweat.

Shoes

Running, turning and braking on court put great strain on your feet. A good pair of shoes is essential to prevent injury.

It is worth buying special tennis shoes for good protection. Don't wear running shoes as they have a thicker sole and are heavier than tennis shoes. Look out for the following features when you are choosing your shoes:

★Good grip on the sole to prevent you slipping.

★Good ventilation.

★Good arch supports to protect your feet.

★Shoes should not be too tight as your feet will expand as they get warm.

★Soft uppers that won't rub and cause soreness or blisters.

★Shoes should be lace-ups to give more support.

★Shoes should be lightweight to put less strain on your feet.

Becoming a professional

Most professional players start off by playing in their school teams. They then work their way up through club and national competitions to international level. There is more about international tennis on pages 34-35.

Not all players, however, follow the same route to the top. For example, some play for their national team while they are still at school. The route you choose depends on your ability, and the advice and support of your coach.

School teams

If you are thinking of a career as a tennis player, it is important to get as much experience of playing matches as possible. A good way to start is by playing for your school team. Your school may also have a coach who will be available for extra practice sessions and team training.

Joining a tennis club

Most areas have local tennis clubs. You can find out about them by contacting your national tennis association or looking in the telephone book.

Some clubs may ask you to 'play in' which means you have to show you are good enough to play for one of their teams. Most clubs, however, are eager to accept junior members.

If possible, try to pick a club with a junior coaching programme. These are usually run at weekends by senior players.

Finding a coach

A good coach is essential if you want your game to progress. Your club should be able to recommend someone to you. You could also ask your national tennis association to send you a list of registered coaches in your area. Book just one lesson to start with, then assess it on the points below before you book any more.

★Do you think you will be able to establish a good, friendly working relationship with the coach?

★Has the coach got plenty of playing and coaching experience to help you develop a sound technique?

★Has the coach a simple, active method of teaching and is he or she likely to make practice sessions fun?

★Will the coach be able to find out about and enter you for local and national tournaments?

A good coach should be tough but encouraging.

Other careers in tennis

Tennis players usually retire quite early, when they are 30-35 years old. Many go on to commentate on tennis for radio or television or become sportswriters. They may also coach or manage other professional players.

Players or people interested in tennis can also sit exams to become umpires or match officials.

It is generally only umpires on the international circuit who get paid.

Entering competitions

Your coach and national tennis association will advise you about tournaments being held locally and nationally. They may also have their own computerized rating scheme. This means they watch you play and give you a score or 'rating' according to how well you do. This will help you pick out tournaments best suited to your standard. As your results improve, so will your ranking, and you will be ready to enter harder competitions.

Turning professional

You may want to earn a living from tennis and become a professional player. Once you have reached the level of national competition, you could progress to the professional tour. You will first have to compete in 'satellite' competitions to earn enough points to get a footing on the world ranking list. You can find out more about these on page 35.

Sponsorship

For players just starting out on an international career, the money needed to cover equipment and travelling expenses can be very off-putting. Many people take part-time jobs to fit around their training.

Another possibility is to approach local businesses and ask if they would sponsor you. For example, many sporting companies allow young players to buy equipment from them at a reduced rate, in return for publicity. Top players are paid huge sums by these companies to use their rackets, clothing and other goods. They may also be offered expensive cars and so on in exchange for the use of their names in advertisements.

Top players have managers to deal with business arrangements.

The rules of tennis

On these two pages there is a summary of the main rules of tennis. Some rules have been explained earlier in the book. The relevant page numbers for these are given in brackets.

Rules 1-2 – the size and shape of the court (see pages 6-7)

Rules 3-4 – the equipment
★Balls must be between 6.35-6.67cm in diameter and weigh between 56.7-58.5g.
 They must not have stitched seams (glue is used instead).
★Rackets must have a flat hitting area and crossed strings attached to the frame.

Rules 5-15 – the service
★At the start of a match, a coin or racket is tossed. The winner of the toss can choose to serve first or which end to receive from.
★The server must stand behind the baseline and between the centre mark and the sideline. The ball must land in the service box diagonally opposite.
★Foot faults (see page 14).
★The server serves alternately from the right and left courts. If he serves from the wrong side by mistake, the point stands but he must serve the next ball from the correct side.
★A service fault is called if:
 – the server misses the ball as he tries to hit it.
 – the ball touches the net and lands out.
 – the ball lands in the wrong service box.
★Second services (see page 15).
★If a 'let' (see page 7) is called, a service or a point is replayed.
★The players must serve alternate games.

Rule 16 – changing ends (see page 33)

Rule 17 – the ball in play
The ball is in play from the moment the service is hit until the point is decided.

Rule 18 – how the server wins points
The server wins a point if:
★the service hits the receiver or his clothing before it hits the ground.
★the receiver loses points as in rule 20.

Rule 19 – how the receiver wins points
The receiver wins a point if:
★the server plays a double fault (see page 15).
★the server loses points as in rule 20.

Rule 20 – how players lose points
Players lose points if:
★the ball bounces twice before they hit it.
★the ball lands out of court (see page 7).
★they catch or carry the ball on their racket or their racket touches the ball more than once when playing a shot.
★their racket or clothing touches the net, the posts, the singles sticks, the net cord or the ground in their opponent's court while the ball is in play.
★they volley the ball before it is on their side of the net.
★the ball touches them or their clothing.
★they throw their racket and hit the ball.

Rule 21 – hindering an opponent
Players lose points if they deliberately prevent opponents playing a stroke. If they accidentally hinder opponents, the point is replayed.

Rule 22 – ball in or out (see page 7)

Rule 23 – ball hitting a fixture
★If the ball hits a permanent fixture (for example, the umpire's chair), other than the net, posts, singles sticks or net cord, after bouncing on court, the player who hit the ball wins the point.

★If the ball hits something before it bounces, the opponent wins the point.

Rule 24 – good returns
A return is good if:
★the ball touches the net, posts, singles sticks or net cord, passes over them and still lands in court.
★the ball goes over the net, bounces or is blown back over and the player whose turn it is to hit the ball reaches over the net and plays the ball (as long as the return is in court).
★a player's racket goes over the net after he has played a shot, provided that he hit the ball on his side of the net.

Rule 25 – being hindered
★If a player is hindered in playing a stroke by something not in his control and not a permanent feature (for example, a ball rolling on to the court, or a bird or animal), or in accordance with rule 21, a 'let' (see page 70) is called.

Rules 26-28 – scoring (see pages 32-33)

Rule 29 – the officials (see page 33)

Rule 30 – continuous play
Play must be continuous from the first service to the end of the match, in accordance with the following rules:
★If the first service is a fault, the server must serve again immediately.
★When changing ends, a maximum of 90 seconds' rest is allowed (see page 33).
★If a player is accidentally injured, the umpire can allow one three-minute break while the injury is treated.
★The warm-up period before a match must not be longer than five minutes.
★The umpire can penalize or disqualify a player for deliberately holding up play.

Rule 31 – coaching
★In some team competitions, a player may receive advice or instructions from the team captain when changing ends.
★Otherwise, coaching is not allowed.

Rule 32 – changing the balls (see page 33)

Rule 33 – doubles rules
The same rules apply for singles and doubles with the exceptions given below.

Rule 34 – the court
The court used for doubles is larger than the singles court (see page 6).

Rule 35 – order of serving
The order of serving may be decided at the beginning of each set.
★The serving pair decide which of them will serve first. The other player serves in their next service game.

Rule 36 – order of receiving
The order of receiving may be decided at the beginning of each set.
★The pair who receive first decide which of them will receive the first service.
★The receiving team receive alternately throughout each game.

Rule 37 – service out of turn
★If the wrong player of a pair serves by mistake, the correct player serves as soon as this is discovered. All points scored before this stand.
★If the game is completed before the mistake is spotted, the order of service stays as altered.

Rule 38 – receiving out of turn
★If the wrong person receives, they go back to the correct order in the next receiving game they play.

Rule 39 – service faults
A service is a fault if the ball touches the server's partner or his clothing (see also rule 10). However, if the ball touches the receiver's partner before it hits the ground, the server wins the point.

Rule 40 – taking turns
The ball must be hit by each team in turn or the point goes to the opponents.

Glossary

Ace A service which is so fast and accurate that an opponent cannot even touch it.

Approach shot A shot, sometimes played with **slice**, which is used to put an opponent on the defensive so you can go forward to the net to **volley**.

Australian formation A tactical doubles formation, where both of the serving team stand on the same side of their half of the court, to stop **cross-court** returns of service.

Backcourt The playing area of the court around the baseline.

Backhand A shot which is played to the left of the body by right-handed players and to the right of the body by left-handed players.

Backswing The action of taking the racket back in preparation for playing a shot.

Ball sense The ability to react quickly to a ball in terms of judging how fast it is moving and where it will bounce.

Baseliner A player with strong, accurate **groundstrokes** who mainly plays long **rallies** from the baseline.

Blocked shot A type of **groundstroke** with a short **backswing**. The racket is 'punched' at the ball after it has bounced. Often used to return fast services.

Breaking the service Winning your opponent's service game or games.

Chipped shot A type of **groundstroke** with a short **backswing** and played with **slice**. Often used to return high, **topspin** services.

Cross-court shot A shot played diagonally across the court.

Deep shot A shot that lands close to the opponent's baseline.

Disguised shot A shot played to surprise an opponent. For example, a player may prepare as if to play a straight **forehand** drive, then play a **drop shot** instead.

Double fault Two services which fail to go into the service box are called a double fault; the opponent wins the point.

Double-handed backhand A **backhand** shot played with both hands holding the racket for extra support, control and power.

Down-the-line shot A shot played straight down a sideline.

Drive A **groundstroke** played on either the **forehand** or **backhand** side.

Drop shot A shot played so that it drops just over the net. Usually played with **slice** so the ball does not bounce high.

Fast court A court with a surface such as grass or cement, which causes the ball to bounce fast. Fast courts tend to suit **serve and volleyers**.

Fault If a service goes into the net or does not land in the correct service court, a fault is called.

Follow-through The racket follows in the direction of the ball after hitting a shot.

Foot fault If the feet touch the baseline or centre line as the ball is served, a foot fault is called. This counts as one **fault**.

Forecourt The playing area of the court between the service line and the net.

Forehand A shot played to the right of the body by a right-handed player and to the left by a left-handed player.

Grip Holding the racket comfortably and with your hand in the best position to hit a particular shot.

Groundstrokes The group of shots played from baseline to baseline with a swinging action. They include **forehand** and **backhand** drives.

Half-volley A difficult shot which is usually played defensively. The ball is hit just after it bounces.

In A ball is said to be 'in' if any part of it lands inside or on the lines marking the boundaries of the court.

Let If a let is called, the point is replayed. A let is called if a service hits the net cord but still lands in the correct service court, or if there is interference during a **rally**.

Lob A shot hit high into the air to clear the opponent's head and land near the opposite baseline.

No man's land The area between the **backcourt** and the **forecourt**. Also called the midcourt.

Out A ball is said to be 'out' if it lands wholly outside the lines marking the boundaries of the court.

Overheads Shots played above your head, such as **smashes**.

Passing shot A shot played past opponents while they are attacking at the net.

Rally An exchange of shots between players. Long **groundstroke** rallies are often played between **baseliners**.

Reflex volley A **volley** in a **rally** at the net which is so fast that it is played purely by instinct.

Serve and volleyer A player who usually serves then immediately runs in to the net to play a **volley**.

Slice Brushing the racket down and under the ball applies slice to a shot. Slice takes the speed off the ball and gives extra control. The ball stays low after bouncing.

Slow court A court with a surface such as clay or tarmac, which causes the ball to bounce slowly and at a steep angle. Slow courts tend to suit **baseliners**.

Smash An overhead shot, played in answer to a **lob**. The ball is hit powerfully downwards into the opponent's half of the court.

Sweet spot The central part of a racket's strings and the best place to hit the ball.

Tandem formation Another name for the **Australian formation** used in doubles play.

Topspin Brushing the racket up and over the ball applies topspin to a shot. Topspin gives speed and extra control. The ball 'kicks' forward after bouncing.

Touch shot A delicate shot, such as a **drop shot**, played with great control rather than power.

Underspin Another name for **slice**.

Unforced error Avoidable mistakes which may lose a player easy points. They may be caused by lack of concentration or loss of control, for example.

Volley A short, quick stroke. The ball is hit before it bounces, with a punching action of the racket.

Wrong footing Playing the ball into a different space from the one you have led your opponent to expect.

Index